LEO

JULY 23 - AUGUST 22

baby

Look out, world !

A Leo was born on _____.

What is my Leo Baby destined to be?

You are clever, cheerful, and charismatic.

You could be a star on TV!

Here's something interesting that you may not know.

Leos radiate confidence wherever they go.

Look at how talented you are!

You'll have so much fun singing on stage for a crowd.

Let's celebrate your accomplishments,

Little Leo.

You are going to make everyone so proud.

You are just like the sun.
You were born to shine bright.

You can conquer all your dreams
with your fiery might.

Do you know
you are a fire sign?

Oh, you love the spotlight!

Others will admire your bravery and strength.

You will only get more courageous as you grow.

With the heart of a lion,
can you imagine where you can go?

Leos are natural-born leaders,

so you are destined to go far.

Always remember,

the world is your stage

and you are the star!

Roar loud,

my mighty lion.

1... 2... 3...

Roarrrr!

Your love for others is so big,

but I love you more.

About the Author

Jen Neary is a Sagittarius
who always felt like she was destined
to be a writer. As the only fire sign in her family,
she was inspired to create this modern
zodiac baby book series for parents and
guardians to learn more about their child's
character traits and unique greatness.

Printed in the USA
CPSIA information can be obtained
at www.ICGtesting.com
LVHW071954081123
763074LV00002B/2